AF266619

The Adventures of Tonsta:
Volume I

Also by Eleanor Currit

The Adventures of Tonsta: Volume II, The
Journey Continues

The Snow Queen's Daughter

The Slain Maiden

The Adventures of Tonsta:

Volume I

Eleanor Currit

For my dad, who read The Hobbit to me when I was sick and inspired a love of Norwegian folk tales.

Contents

***

Tonsta and the Hag

A long time ago, in the old country, there was a comely widow who had four sons, each more accomplished and clever than the next. The youngest, a lad named Tonsta, was the cleverest of all.

Every day when his brothers left to chop wood in the forest, or tend to the goats, he would sit at his mother's scrubbed kitchen table tinkering with tools and toys. He was always taking things apart and fixing them. When his brothers would return for supper, they would ask what he had done that day, and when he showed them some new contraption he had invented, they would jeer at him. Their mother didn't always understand what Tonsta was doing, though she would smile and nod proudly whenever he showed her what he'd built. However, Tonsta was never discouraged.

One day in late fall, as Tonsta was sitting at the table repairing a gadget he had affixed to his knife, a heavily cloaked stranger came hobbling up to their door. A very old woman, the stranger's skin had a mossy tinge to it, and her face looked more like the rings of a tree stump, than wrinkles. She was also very tall, much too tall for the short roof of the house. Tonsta didn't much like the look of her, and stowing his knife in his britches, he hid himself in the cupboard.

"Good day, friend," Mother said, swishing her long flaxen braid over her shoulder and picking up her laundry basket. She eyed the stranger warily.

"Good day!" the old woman replied, with a voice that was reminiscent of the time Tonsta threw marbles in his mother's wheat grinder. "Might you spare a bowl of stew for a poor wanderer?"

Being a good Christian woman, Mother invited the stranger in for a morsel, and the odd-looking person hunched her back even more to enter the shack. The crone sat at the table, and the stool groaned beneath her weight, and she eyed the tools Tonsta had left on the table.

"From whence do you come?" Mother asked.

"From yonder forest, and beyond. Have you a husband at home?" the old woman asked.

Now, Mother was a good Christian woman who believed lying was wrong, but she also knew better than to divulge too much information to strangers.

"He's out back chopping wood," Mother said, with nary a hint of falsehood. "I expect he'll be home soon."

She placed a steaming bowl before the stranger and began to fold the garments from the clothesline. The crone slurped loudly at the stew, her eyes, like a pair of shiny beetles, sweeping the tiny cottage. She sniffed deeply, as though her nose was dripping.

"Are your children at home?" she asked.

Mother's neck stiffened a little, but she kept on folding with a look on unconcern on her face.

"I have no children."

The old woman didn't seem to believe her but didn't press the point.

"I have a son," she commented in her gravelly voice. "A comely lad, with arms like tree trunks."

"He sounds like a fine lad," Mother replied, in a tone which invited no further conversation.

The crone finished her stew, thanked Mother, and departed.

As soon as the stranger was out of sight, Mother summoned Tonsta from the cupboard and sent him to fetch his brothers for supper.

"But keep a look out for the wanderer, and don't let her catch sight of you," she warned.

Tonsta found his brothers quickly enough, since they were already walking back, and from the same direction that the wanderer had gone.

"Did you pass an evil looking old hag?" Tonsta asked, as soon as they were within earshot.

The eldest brother cuffed Tonsta about the ear and said, "We saw naught but a sickly old woman!" and the other two brothers guffawed appreciatively.

Tonsta sulked in the corner through supper, sharpening his little knife, while his brothers told their mother of the goings-on in town.

"Tomorrow I'd like you to take the goats to the stream to graze," Mother said.

The boys protested. The stream was in the opposite direction from town, and a much more difficult trek, they insisted. Tonsta knew the only reason they cared about town was the Earl's flaxen-haired daughter. Mother insisted, however, so the following day as the brothers set out with bread and cheese in their pockets, they led the goats toward the foot of the mountain instead of town.

No sooner had the brothers disappeared from sight than the old woman from the day before appeared, shambling up the hill looking more like some drifting stump than a woman.

"Hide yourself away," Mother told Tonsta, gathering all his tools and toys in her apron and stowing it in the ash heap.

Tonsta leapt up from the table obediently and skipped off to the cupboard. But in such a hurry was he that his little red cap fell off his head and landed on the hearth.

The crone came up to the door and knocked with her gnarled fist. Slowly, and with a grace that befitted a lady, Mother answered the door.

"Good day, friend," Mother said. "What brings you to my cottage?"

The old woman leaned heavily on a walking stick, which was as knobbly and gnarled as her hands, and scrutinized Mother with her beady eyes.

"Might you spare a scrap of bread for a poor old woman?"

Mother, being a good Christian woman, welcomed her in, shooting a cautious look at the cupboard to be sure Tonsta was out of sight.

The old woman tore away noisily at the bread and cheese Mother set before her and swept the cottage with a greedy gaze.

"Where have you come from, friend?" Mother asked.

"From yonder mountain and beyond," the crone replied. "Have you a husband at home?" she asked, her eyes spying the red cap on the hearth.

"He's out back milking the goats," Mother said, with nary a hint of deceit.

The old crone harrumphed and swallowed the last piece of bread. She sniffed at the air as though smelling something foul.

"Where are your sons?" she asked, eyeing Mother as though she would see them reflected in her eyes.

"I have no sons," Mother replied, shrugging.

The old crone got to her feet and leaned on her stick once more.

"I have a son. He's a good lad, with hair as thick as tree moss and eyes that match his dark soul."

"He sounds like a fine lad," Mother replied, with a finality that invited no further discourse.

The old crone departed, limping down the hill with a speed that seemed unlikely for her. Mother had a slight frown on her face when she came to fetch Tonsta. Tonsta reached for his cap, but Mother shook her head.

"I want you to follow the old woman for a spell, but don't let yourself be seen, then come back and tell me where she's gone."

Well, Tonsta had to run a little to catch up, for the crone was a good deal faster than her deportment let on. Once he did, he hunkered down and dashed from bush to bush. He followed her until the sun hung low on the sky, but when he finally lost track of her he turned around and went home.

"Well?" Mother asked, when Tonsta returned, with twigs and leaves sticking in his hair and clothing.

"She followed the path till the bottom of the hill," Tonsta said, shaking the moss out of his boot. "Then she turned off sharply and made straight for the mountain."

Mother's face was very serious indeed, but she said no more on the matter, and set to work preparing dinner. When the brothers returned that night, Tonsta again asked if they had seen the old woman. The second eldest took hold of Tonsta's cap and pulled it down over his eyes.

"We saw a crippled old woman struggling up the mountain," the older boy said. "Are you afraid of your shadow too, or just old women?" and the other brothers laughed and clapped Tonsta on the back, causing him to slosh his warm milk.

No sooner had the brothers departed the following day than the old woman was knocking at the door with her walking stick.

"Quick, into the cupboard," Mother said. "Good day," she greeted the old woman.

"Good day," growled the wanderer. "Might you spare a bite for an old woman?"

Mother set a board of bread and goat cheese before the old woman and set to kneading the dough she had started. The crone peered about the kitchen, her evil eyes resting on the cupboard.

"Where have you come from today?" Mother asked.

The crone gave her a look so sharp it could have sliced cheese.

"Here and there," she replied. "Have you a husband?"

"He's in the chicken coop, I'm surprised you didn't hear him singing as he worked," Mother said, without a hint of deceit. The crone grunted indifferently. She sniffed at the air, loudly and with a look of deep disgust.

"Where are your sons?" she asked.

"I have no children," Mother replied.

"I have a son," the old woman rumbled. "He's as tall as a tree, and just as thick, but he's obedient."

Mother smiled coolly, dusting flour onto her apron.

"He sounds like a fine lad," she said.

"And *you* will make him a fine wife!" the hag cried, tossing back her hood and revealing her mossy head. Quick as a cat, the troll leapt to her feet, knocking the stool aside, and threw a giant sack over Mother's head.

Mother shouted and wriggled, but the troll hag gave the bag a sharp rap with her walking stick, and the sack stopped moving. Poor little Tonsta didn't know what to do! When the troll hag knocked over the stool, it had become lodged in front of the cupboard, and no matter how hard he pushed, he couldn't escape. So, he watched helplessly through a crack as the troll trudged away, with his Mother slung over its shoulder like a sack of potatoes! Tonsta kicked at the door until he was exhausted and his cheeks were pink with exertion.

Finally, long after it had gone dark outside the cupboard, Tonsta heard the sounds of his brothers returning. They entered the cottage shouting for their mother and asking why they didn't smell supper. Of course, they heard Tonsta kicking at the cupboard door and let him out, much to their amusement.

At first, they refused to believe that the haggard old woman they had passed on the path could have kidnapped their mother, but after much discussion and stamping of feet, they heard Tonsta out. After that, they had to decide what to do.

The eldest suggested that they go to the Earl and ask him to gather his men, to hunt down the creature, but Tonsta insisted there was no time.

The next suggested that he go alone to track the troll and slay it himself. No one liked this idea much, so they agreed on all going together to rescue their mother. Tonsta grabbed his little tool belt and a length of rope and puffed out his chest as he waited by the door, but his brothers only scoffed.

"You're not coming," they told him, and when he protested, they picked him up by the arms and stuffed him back in the cupboard, jamming the door once more.

Tonsta stuck out his lip and scowled, but he refused to cry.

"I'm not a baby," he told himself. "I just need to get out of this cupboard, and I'll hunt that troll down by myself!"

He had any number of tools in his little belt, but he went with the simplest, and set to work with his hammer, knocking the pins out of the hinges. They were old and rusted, and it took Tonsta quite a bit longer than he had imagined, and by the time he had removed the door and crawled out, his brothers were nowhere in sight.

He pulled his little red cap over his ears and set off, following the obvious trail left by his brothers. It was bitterly cold, and the only light Tonsta had to go by was the moon, but "It's just as well. I don't want to alert every creature on the mountain," he thought.

He walked, and walked, until his feet ached, and the cold had turned the muddy prints he was following to ice. Just as he was beginning to tire and the sun was beginning to rise, he came to an ancient stone staircase. It was overgrown by moss and dusted with recent snow. At the top of the stairs was a heavy double door, set right into the cliff.

"Humph," Tonsta said, scratching his head a little, and glaring at the problem. He had brought a climbing hook on a length of rope, as well as a set of lock picks, and he inspected the door carefully, looking for a handle or keyhole, but there was no visible way to open it.

There seemed to be only one way forward, a way that would get him caught, which was most certainly the point. He reached up and knocked on the door as loudly as he could, then dashed under a bush to hide. There was a loud shuffling sound from the other side of the door before it opened, and the ugliest face Tonsta had ever seen peered out.

It could be no one other than the troll hag's son, for she had spoken truly when she said he was built like a thick tree, although she had left out the resemblance his nose bore to a turnip. His head was covered in a mane of what must have been hair, but looked more like lichen, and his eyes were hidden behind a curtain of the stuff.

The troll swiveled his head about stupidly for a moment or two, then turned to shamble back inside. Quick as a whip and quiet as a mouse, Tonsta dashed through the door and hid in the lumbering creature's shadow. Beyond the door was a large courtyard, which Tonsta was surprised to find was open to the sky, since trolls fear sunlight. Beyond that was a castle. It was covered in what must have been centuries of moss, and tree roots had broken through much of the stone work, crumbling it. Whatever this place had been, the stronghold of some ancient kingdom perhaps, the mountain was reclaiming it.

There was a pile of rotting barrels just inside the gate and Tonsta jumped inside one, using it to follow the troll without being spotted. He doubted very much whether the troll would notice a barrel out of place, but he froze and covered his toes every time the creature turned, nonetheless.

He hoped very much that he was following the troll to wherever the creatures had imprisoned Mother, for he had no doubt it would take a full day to explore the entire castle, and who knew what sort of danger she was in. Tonsta was also beginning to suspect his brothers were prisoners as well, for he had seen no evidence of them since the bottom of the steps.

The troll led him down several corridors and a flight of steps, and more than once he paused to sniff the air with a look of confusion. Tonsta had begun to sweat inside the barrel, but he hoped the troll would simply assume he was smelling the other human prisoners.

Finally, troll and barrel both shuffled into the dungeon. Tonsta crept sideways into the room, trying to camouflage himself in the dark corner while the troll lit a torch. The creature started making a grunting, growling sound, as he picked up a bucket and heaved it toward one of the cells, slopping some unrecognizable mush at the bars. It took Tonsta a full minute to realize the troll was speaking, but he couldn't make out a single word. He waited until the sounds of the troll dragging his feet had died off, before removing his barrel and approaching the cells.

"Mother?" he called out softly.

The prisoner stirred at the sound of Tonsta's voice and crept forward cautiously. Tonsta's heart sank as he saw that the prisoner was not Mother, or even one of his brothers, but instead a red fox, wearing trousers. It cocked its head at him curiously.

"No, no!" it exclaimed, in a voice as smooth as silk. "This isn't where you want to be, child. Flee! Flee while you still can."

Now, Tonsta would have liked to ask how a fox came to be speaking, wearing trousers, and locked in a troll's dungeon, but there was no time for such things.

"The troll hag has kidnapped my mother, and plans to marry her to that dimwitted, vile son of hers. My brothers came to rescue her, but I haven't seen any sign of them either!"

The fox switched its tail and pawed at the cell door.

"If you let me out, I will help you find them. I know this castle well, for I came in search of a treasure said to be buried beneath it, but I was captured before I could make off with it. You'll find the keys on the troll hag's belt, but how you'll get them I do not know." He looked Tonsta up and down uncertainly, as though doubtful he was up to the challenge.

"I don't need them!" Tonsta declared, and reaching into his little tool belt, he dug out the lock picks. "But how do I know you'll live up to your end?" He had always been told that foxes were sly and not to be trusted.

The fox looked mildly injured and tucked one paw back as he bowed his head, which gave him a courtly, slightly ridiculous look.

"On my honor," the fox said. "Which, among *my own* people is a good as gold."

Tonsta apologized for offending the fox and set to work on the lock. It was very rusty, and more complicated than any lock Tonsta had ever picked before, but he managed, and in short order the door was swinging open and the fox trotted out.

"I do apologize for my scent, friend," the fox intoned regretfully. "Trolls aren't in the habit of cleaning their cells or giving their prisoners the opportunity to wash themselves."

"That's quite alright," Tonsta replied, his eyes watering a little. "Where do you suppose they're keeping my mother and brothers?"

"The north tower, I would stake my life on it. I spotted some cages hanging in there when I entered, although at the time they were empty."

So, the fox led Tonsta toward the north tower, leaving Tonsta's barrel behind for the sake of speed. They saw no one on the way, although several times they heard the shuffling steps of the trolls nearby. When they reached the north tower, the fox pointed at a small hole in the wall.

"Here is where I suggest you make your entry."

"You're not coming with me?" Tonsta asked, slightly miffed.

"I have my own mission to complete," the fox said, winking. "But when I make my escape, I shall be sure to make enough racket that I draw the trolls far from you. Give your mother my regards and tell her she raised a fine lad." He bowed again, looking very grand in his weather worn old trousers, and slunk away.

Tonsta sighed and getting down on his belly he squirmed through the hole. His tool belt got stuck on the way, and he untied it and pulled it through behind him. He peered about the room as he put his belt back on and as his eyes adjusted they were drawn high up to the ceiling. Sure enough, just as the fox had said, there were cages hanging from the ceiling, and in those cages, were his brothers.

When they espied him, they began to shout and cry for joy, but Tonsta scowled and held a finger up to his lips until they quieted down. The height of the cages presented a problem, for even if Tonsta had been a grown man, he wouldn't have been able to reach them. He swept the room with his gaze for a moment, until his eyes rested on the chandelier. Climbing on a broken old table, Tonsta got out his rope and grappling hook and began to swing it. Seeing the shiny hook, the brothers protested and threw out other suggestions, but when Tonsta released the hook it found its mark on the chandelier and stayed fast even as he gave it a good yank. He began the arduous climb up the rope, holding his lock pick in his teeth. When he finally reached the height of the cages, he began to swing until he managed to grab hold of one and work his way around to the door.

The lock went quickly and Tonsta let his brother down the rope as he started on the next lock. When the eldest brother, who was by no means a small boy, jumped down to the floor, it let out an awful cracking, splintering sound.

Just as the last brother was sliding down the rope, they heard the jangle of keys at the door.

"Quick through the hole!" Tonsta called down, for he was still hanging from the middle of the ceiling.

The brothers all dashed for the hole, pushing each other through in their haste. The last one had just squeezed through, snapping a few buttons, as the door burst open to reveal the troll hag's son. He stared up at the cages for a moment or two before he seemed to realize they were empty, then he let out a bellow of anger. He spotted Tonsta, perched on the chandelier with his feet hanging down, and looking as cool as a cucumber.

"You! You steal! Thief!" Tonsta managed to make out, and he wondered if the fox had managed to make off with the treasure he was seeking. The troll sputtered on the spot angrily and gestured at him. As tall as he was, the troll couldn't reach him, Tonsta realized with glee.

He waited until the troll had quieted down a bit before calling out in his own squeaky little voice, "If you want your treasure back, you'll just have to come up and get it from me."

The troll considered this for a moment, and Tonsta imagined the wheels turning in his head behind that curtain of hair. The troll turned and stalked out of the room very suddenly, and Tonsta wondered if he had gone to get his mother, who seemed by far the cleverer of the two. However, a moment later he came back in, pushing ahead of him a great stone block, which once must have been part of the castle. There was a look of triumph on his great, stupid face. He pushed the stone into the center of the room, directly beneath Tonsta. The floor creaked ominously.

"Well come on then!" Tonsta shouted. "I can't wait around all day." Behind the troll, he could see the uncertain faces of his brothers peeking out from behind the rubble of the castle.

The troll lurched forward, clambering up the stone. The floor creaked, but remained intact, and with a cackle of glee the troll reached up and swiped at Tonsta's toes. Holding the end of the rope firmly, and saying a prayer, Tonsta jumped from the chandelier and landed on the stone in front of the troll. The floor groaned. Before the troll could realize what had happened, the wood buckled beneath the weight of stone, troll, and little boy. The stone block shot through the floor, taking the troll with it, and leaving Tonsta dangling.

As it happened, that wooden floor was all that lay between the room and the open sky, and for all we know, the troll hag's son might still be falling to this day.

Tonsta swung towards the door, and his brothers managed to grab hold of him and bring him in safely.

"Now to rescue mother!" the eldest said. Tonsta would very much have liked to point out that it was he who had done all the rescuing up to this point, but he kept that to himself.

The brothers said they had only seen the troll hag and her son, who was now gone, and given the state of the castle they had no reason to suspect anyone else lived there. Still, they wandered with caution, certain at any moment they would come upon the troll hag.

They came to a great set of doors, which seemed as though they had been very finely decorated once upon a time but were now rotted. They pushed the doors open cautiously and found themselves in a throne room, destroyed by time and nature, but a throne room nonetheless.

The middle brother gasped and pointed, and they all froze as they spotted what he was looking at. Sitting on the throne, as still as a statue, and as hideous as her son, was the troll hag. It took even Tonsta a moment to realize she was sitting *too* still. She had turned to stone. Tonsta glanced at the windows as he cautiously approached. It was a very overcast day; it had even begun to snow. At the foot of the throne lay a small crystal ball, no bigger than Tonsta's fist. Beside it, scratched in the thick layer of dust was a single word; 'regards.' Tonsta grinned to himself as he remembered the fox's words.

Tonsta picked up the ball and very nearly dropped it again as it suddenly grew warm. He held it up to the light it and began to glow, becoming so bright he could no longer look at it. He slipped it into his tool belt, blinking and seeing spots.

Certain now that there was no more danger, they explored deeper into the castle, calling out for their mother, until they heard a shout back. Following the sound, they came to the bottom of a locked stairwell.

"If only we had taken the keys from the hag!" the brothers grumbled. "Now we shall have to go all the way back."

"Have you learned nothing today?" Tonsta scolded them, and he had the door unlocked in a snap.

Quite the opposite of her sons, Mother had been well cared for and fed, although she had spent her time scratching away at the wall with a spoon. Well, of course they were all overjoyed to be reunited, and Mother was amazed to hear all that had transpired. She would not believe it until she saw the stone hag, and the gaping hole for herself.

Tonsta told them what the fox had said about treasure, and his brothers insisted on searching the entire castle again, but although they searched it twice more, they never found any treasure.

"Well at least I have this in case any troll bothers us again," Tonsta said patting his tool belt where he had stowed the glowing ball.

They returned home, and although they were none the richer by the experience, Tonsta hoped that his family had a new respect for him. Mother prepared dinner, and his brothers told her again how they had vanquished the troll, and Tonsta worked on his tools, and all was right with the world.

Tonsta and the Chicken Snatcher

After the spring rains, when the fjord had begun to thaw, Tonsta decided it was time for him to go out and see the world. Mother vehemently protested, "After all," she said, "you've only just turned ten." But Tonsta's brothers reminded her of how well he had handled the trolls the previous fall, and Mother was forced to admit that was true.

"Never fear," Tonsta said, cheerily patting his tool satchel. "I have the magic ball that holds the sun, that the fox left. If I run into any trouble, I can quickly dispatch any trolls I meet."

So Tonsta packed a little sack, and stuffed it with his mother's cooking, and every tool and trick he could think of, and set off. He received quite a number of stares as he strolled through town, for although he wasn't well known for playing with other children, many people had heard stories of

the eccentric little red-capped son of the fair
widow.

Tonsta had never been far from home. His
adventure the previous year had been quite an
anomaly, therefore the forest on the other side of
town seemed like quite an intimidating place. As
night fell, and it began to get chilly, Tonsta began
to think longingly of starting a fire, but it had been
drizzling all day and he was unlikely to find dry
wood. Therefore, he kept walking in hopes of
finding shelter. It felt like he had been marching
half the night away before he finally saw a cave,
and when he did, it was less than ideal.

Tonsta's eldest brother had told him that this
forest was supposed to be full of caves, but his
words had been spoken in warning, not
recommendation. However, when Tonsta saw the
drippy, mossy opening of a cave beside the stream
he'd been following, he threw caution to the wind
and ducked inside. He shivered and did a dance on

the spot as a drip found its way down the back of his tunic.

As his eyes adjusted to the dark, Tonsta let out a cry of delight, for he saw the remnants of an old fire, which would most certainly be dry down here, away from the rain.

He settled down next to it and was all set to get it crackling once more, when a voice like the sound of falling rocks emanated from deeper within the cave.

"What do you think you're doing?"

If Tonsta hadn't already been chilled to the bone, then having a disembodied voice talk to him in a dark cave most certainly would have done the trick. He cleared his throat and replied as confidently as he could in his squeaky young voice.

"Please, my good man, if you are a man, and I do hope so with a voice like yours. I would just like to get the fire going. I imagine you must be almost as cold as I am on a night like this.

Assuming, that is, that you aren't a spirit of some sort."

There was a scraping, rumbling sound, and a heaping figure emerged from the back of the cave. It was still too dark to see, but from the general shape, the voice, and the smell, Tonsta assumed it was a troll.

"But seeing as how you aren't in the most welcoming mood, I suppose I'll just have to brighten you up!" With that, Tonsta drew the magic sun ball from his tool satchel and held it up. Nothing happened.

The troll chuckled, with a sound like someone chewing rocks, and sat down by the fire with a loud 'thump', shaking the ground a little.

"Nice toy," he said. "But it seems someone forgot to leave you the instruction manual, my lad. Odin's Eye doesn't work unless there is daylight to absorb, and as you can see…" He waved a shovel sized hand at the dark cave.

"Is that what it's called?" Tonsta replied, trying to remain calm in the face of this snag. "I've just been calling it a glow ball."

"How *imaginative* of you," the troll sniffed.

"As you say, friend, I was given no instruction with it," Tonsta replied, hoping that if he kept the troll amiable enough, he might still leave this cave alive and perhaps learn more about this 'Odin's Eye'.

"Who *did* give it to you, by the way?" the troll asked, in what he must have assumed was a smooth, inviting tone.

Now, Tonsta was a good Christian lad, who didn't like to lie if it wasn't necessary, and given that the fox had never actually told him his name, he didn't see the harm in being truthful.

"A fox in trousers," he replied.

He expected another burst of laughter from his companion, however, the troll accepted this rather seriously. It took the troll a while to respond, and after a long moment, he replied with forced tranquility.

"How… interesting," he commented. "I don't suppose you know the name of this trouser-wearing fox?"

"Haven't the foggiest," Tonsta replied.

"A pity," the troll said. "Well I suppose there's nothing for it now but to eat you."

Tonsta felt like he'd swallowed a large rock, but he did his best to maintain his unruffled attitude.

"Now, now," he said. "That seems a bit of an overreaction. After all what have I really done? I wandered into what I thought was an empty cave, and I've done my best to answer your questions."

The troll made a sound like 'hah', and Tonsta guessed he was scoffing at him. He supposed he couldn't blame the troll for that; after all, he had tried to use the glow ball on him.

"You disturbed my nap and tried to turn me to stone!" the troll intoned irately.

"Perhaps we can agree, things were said and done on both sides?" Tonsta suggested. He was greeted by a wall of silence. "I at least deserve a chance to win my way out of being eaten. Surely you consider yourself a fair fellow?"

The troll sighed deeply, a sound like a gust of wind.

"Very well," he agreed. "If you can answer me three questions, I won't eat you."

Tonsta thought that seemed fair and agreed.

"Might I make a fire? I'm chilled to the bone and if I lose, I'm assuming you won't want to eat me raw."

The troll saw the wisdom in this and told Tonsta he could make his fire. So, he set to work, and soon he had a merry blaze going to warm himself, and he could also see his unpleasant companion.

As trolls go, they're all ugly and typically have an attitude to match, but this troll looked as though he had gone through a mill and managed to come out the other side in one piece. His face was covered in scars which suggested it had once been sliced to ribbons, and one of his eyes was cloudy. His carrot-like nose was missing a gash or two of flesh.

Tonsta took all this in without a word and smiled as pleasantly as he could at a creature who wanted to eat him.

"So, now that we're both dry and comfortable, what questions will I be answering?"

The troll grinned, at least that was what Tonsta assumed, for his perpetually downturned mouth was so deformed it could barely form any other shape.

"Firstly, how old am I? Secondly, what is my name? And lastly, how was I given that name?"

Tonsta listened carefully and took off his little red cap to dry over the fire. The troll waited for him to speak, and it was hard to tell, but Tonsta felt certain that the troll had a gleeful look in his good eye.

"May I round up or down on your age?"

The troll considered a moment then nodded.

"Might I tell you a story while I consider my answers?" Tonsta asked.

The troll looked at him suspiciously, a small glimmer of doubt on the plowed field he considered a face, but all trolls love a good story.

"I suppose but make it quick. The fire is making me drowsy and I don't want to sleep on an empty stomach."

"Very well," Tonsta gulped, then cleared his throat and began. "When I was very young, my grandmother would tell me a story, that *her* grandmother told her. For the sake of time, let's just say my grandmother is the grandmother I'll describe in the telling of this tale?"

The troll looked muddled but nodded anyway.

"When "my" grandmother was a young woman, she and grandpapa raised chickens on a farm near the mountains. Meat hens, egg layers, they all thrived and the rooster kept them well and safe.

"Well one day, when grandpapa had gone to a nearby town for a few days, grandmother noticed one or two of the hens were missing, as was the rooster. At first, she supposed martens had stolen them. But she checked every nook and cranny of the chicken coop and there was no way for them to have slipped in and out, especially with hens as fat as theirs! The following night it happened again."

The troll had a queasy look on his face, but he didn't interrupt as Tonsta continued.

"She realized that whoever, or whatever, had taken the chickens must have opened the door. Without grandpapa at home and the rooster missing, grandmother was worried about losing more hens. So, she went over to the neighboring farm to see if they had a rooster, but all they had to give her was a runty looking little thing. It didn't even look big enough to intimidate some of the larger hens! Grandmother was certain the farmer was cheating her by selling her such a small, ugly rooster, but it was the best she could do, so she brought it home."

The troll looked ready to spring from his seat, so tense was his body. His good eye was glaring at Tonsta and his teeth were bared. But Tonsta continued nonetheless.

"That night my grandmother was awoken by a racket you wouldn't believe coming from the henhouse. It sounded as though someone were dying! The hens were making a commotion as well. So, grandmother grabbed the ax by the door and went out in her nightgown to see what was happening. What she saw made tears of laughter roll down her cheeks! The runty little rooster she had bought that day was latched onto a young troll, who was yowling and dancing on the spot, trying to dislodge the thing while it took swipes at his face with its spurs. The neighbors were awaked by the noise as well, and everyone who lived in the area came to see what the commotion was about, and everyone laughed. Now, my grandmother was a good Christian woman, and had compassion on the young troll. So, despite the flying spurs and dancing troll, she got in there and pried the rooster off.”

The troll sitting across from Tonsta looked like he was ready to leap across the campfire and throttle him. So infuriated was he that he hadn’t noticed the first rays of daylight shining outside the cave.

“By the time grandmother got the rooster off, the poor troll’s face was sliced to ribbons, as were the clothes on his back. Now rescued from the rooster, but being stared at and laughed at instead, the troll took off running into the night. He was seen from time to time after that, stealing food here and there, but he never stole chickens again.

"So, to answer your questions, you're just about three hundred years old. Humans call you Tatter-face, but your own kind call you Chick-feed, because you were bested by a chicken. In conclusion, I believe I just explained *how* you got your name!"

The troll shrieked like steam coming out of a kettle.

"You cheated!" he spat in his rage. "You lit the fire to see me!"

Tonsta shrugged, reaching surreptitiously into his tool satchel and feeling about without lowering his gaze.

"I played fairly, friend, now I must insist you do the same."

"Pah! Fairly…" the troll seethed. "It doesn't matter, I'll still eat you."

"I think not!" Tonsta cried and held up the Odin's Eye to catch the daylight outside the cave.

It flashed blindingly and Tonsta squeezed his eyes shut, seeing spots. After a minute he felt safe putting the thing away, and he cracked an eye open cautiously. The troll was frozen in a rather frightening pose, half risen, as though he were about to swoop down on the boy. Tonsta shivered.

He couldn't help but feel a bit sorry for the troll; after all, Tatter-face must have had a hard three centuries with a story like that following him about. On the other hand, he had been downright gleeful at the prospect of eating Tonsta. Despite his humble condition, as it turned out, Tatter-face had quite a substantial amount of gold in his purse, and Tonsta went ahead and added that to his own satchel.

He pulled his little red cap over his ears, slung his sack over his shoulder, and carried on his way.

One day in early summer, Tonsta came upon a small village where the houses were all painted bright cheerful colors, but the townspeople watched him with suspicious, fearful eyes.

He made his way to the inn and bought a hot meal where he received even more stares for the giant gold coin he paid with.

"Excuse me, my good man," Tonsta called out to the innkeeper. "No offense intended, but I cannot help but notice the unfriendly air in this village."

The innkeeper grunted and looked up and down the bar as though afraid to be caught speaking to his own customer.

"This used to be the friendliest, liveliest town north of the Razor," the man told Tonsta in a lowered tone. Tonsta assumed the 'Razor' must be the knife shaped peak he had seen in the distance the last few days. "But a few months back, strange things began happening in the area. The miller's daughter went out to milk the cow, but instead of milk, she came back with a pail of gold string! Things like that began to happen every few days after that and at first, we thought it was a gift. Everyone grew wealthier. I tapped a barrel to find it full of unmarked gold coins; enough to fix up the roof and more! But then one night, there was a frightful storm, thunder and lightning. In that storm, it began to hail, not ice, but gold nuggets the size of a man's fist! It destroyed the newly built roof, and many others besides, and a man was knocked unconscious. It was then we realized that this was no gift; we are cursed!"

"Intriguing!" Tonsta exclaimed. "I would very much like to witness some such strange occurrence before I go on my way. But that doesn't explain why the townspeople are treating strangers with such caution."

"Well," the innkeeper wiped down the gleaming bar in front of the young boy, glancing sideways at a group in the corner, who were scowling at him. "The question is, who cursed us! Once we all agreed it was a curse, we thought back to the week it started. A strange looking little fellow came through town, asking all sorts of funny questions about the ruins out east."

Tonsta's ear prickled.

"An odd-looking fellow you say? Rather like a walking stump perhaps, towering above the roof?"

"He was a short fellow," the man insisted. "No taller than you, lad. Although with a voice like his, there was no doubt in my mind he was a man."

This surprised Tonsta, for he had yet to see a small troll.

"What of his face?"

The innkeeper stroked his beard thoughtfully.

"I couldn't rightly tell you what his face looked like. He wore a dark hood you see. But after that, we all suspected the little fellow of bringing the curse. We even sent a band of our finest young men out to the ruins, to hunt him down, and demand he lift the curse. They came back empty handed, insisting that some ghost had been awakened in the ruins."

Aha! Tonsta thought. This was most certainly his sort of problem.

"Tell me of the ruins?" Tonsta asked excitedly.

The innkeeper wiped a bead of sweat from his lip and blinked nervously.

"It is the ruin of an ancient castle, buried by time. Now only one tower remains standing, although it is believed the rest is still intact beneath the ground. They say if you walk by it at night you can hear the ghosts crying out for vengeance on the descendants of those who killed them."

"I don't believe in ghosts!" Tonsta declared, only somewhat truthfully. "I shall travel to this ruin, and find who cast this curse, then I will make them lift it."

Tonsta must have sounded quite amusing making such claims, for the innkeeper, as well as the scowling group in the corner, burst out laughing. Seeing the miffed look on Tonsta's face, the innkeeper composed himself and shook his head.

"Nay lad, your head barely reaches the bar; how could you hope to battle spirits?"

Tonsta stood up and pushed back his stool, puffing his chest out and scowling.

"I *will* vanquish this curse, and if I do, *you* and everyone in this town will owe me the worth of repairing your roof!" He held out his hand, and reluctantly, still chuckling a little, the innkeeper shook it, sealing the agreement.

"Very well, lad. I hope for your sake the ghosts aren't hungry."

Heaving his bag back over his shoulder, Tonsta headed out of the village, to the east, where he had been told the ruins lay. Very soon, he began to hear a strange noise. The closer he got to the ruins, the louder it became, and the more certain he became that it wasn't an animal.

The tower sat in the midst of a thicket, with no other visible buildings nearby, and the sound was most definitely emanating from within. Tonsta listened to the long moaning voice for a moment hoping to distinguish words, but when he could not, he called out.

"Friend! What troubles you?"

The moaning ceased, but in its absence Tonsta picked up another sound, one he couldn't quite place. Suddenly, something small and hard collided with the top of Tonsta's head, followed quickly by a few more. He looked up at the sky and instantly regretted it as a shower of tiny golden pebbles rained down on his face. It was showering gold!

"Well I *did* say I wanted to witness it for myself," Tonsta said to himself irritably, rubbing his nose.

"Who's there?" A gravelly, frightened voice sounded from within the tower.

"A friend seeking shelter from this torrent," Tonsta replied.

There was a long silence and Tonsta looked at the tiny window in the tower, expecting to see a face poking out. Finally, the voice responded, sounding weary and resigned.

"I hope you can climb," was all it said.

Sighing, Tonsta tied his little sack about his neck and inspected the stones of the tower. They seemed large enough to grip. Near the top, he dared to glance down.

"Well, that wasn't nearly as far as I thought it was!" He peered in the window and stifled a laugh.

He wasn't quite sure what he'd been expecting, but the sight that met his eyes had certainly never occurred to him. The floor was completely covered in a fine gold thread, and at the center of the room, seated at a spinning wheel, was a pair of forlorn black eyes, staring out of the golden snarl.

"Finally!" the spinner exclaimed. "Be a good lad and get me out of this."

Tonsta bit back his laugh and folded his arms, taking in the scene.

"I might be persuaded," he said. "But first, tell me how you got into such a predicament."

The spinner scowled, or at least that's what Tonsta assumed from the way his eyes moved, but he launched into the story anyway.

As it happened, there was quite the legend surrounding the castle and the downfall of its inhabitants. But I won't get into that just now. Suffice it to say, the spinner had learned that there was an enchanted object in the castle, which would grant you unimaginable wealth. He had come to the town seeking information on the legends, and upon realizing the townspeople knew nothing, he had simply broken into the castle to have a look.

The spinner had expected to have a difficult time finding and identifying the object, but when he climbed through the window, the spinning wheel was sitting right there, looking clean and untouched by age. So, of course he had sat down and set to work.

"And that's when I finally understood the legend," the spinner whined. He shook what must have been his arm, underneath the piles of gold thread. "The moment I sat down, my hair turned to gold and grew, tying me to this seat and forcing me to continue spinning! All I wanted was a treasure, now I just want out of this tower."

Tonsta nodded solemnly, thinking of the cautionary tales his mother had always told him about the love of gold.

"What can I do?" Tonsta asked. "How does one stop the spinning wheel?"

"Burn it!" the spinner cried, his eyes popping a little.

"That seems a bit extreme, doesn't it?" Tonsta frowned.

"Ohh!" The spinner wailed, and the gentle tinkle of golden rain on the roof grew louder. "You do not know the anguish I'm in, or you would not ask such a ridiculous question! To be stuck to this chair for so long…why, I can't feel my feet anymore! Burn the whole tower down if you must, just release me!"

"All right, all right, calm down!" Tonsta glanced anxiously out the window at the worsening weather.

He approached the quivering pile of gold cautiously, stepping gingerly to avoid tripping in the snarl of thread. He dug around for a few moments until the spinning wheel was more accessible, then retrieved his little tinder box. But try as he might, he couldn't light the enchanted spinning wheel.

"What's taking so long?" the spinner demanded.

"It won't light," Tonsta declared.

The spinner made a grumbling sound like an avalanche.

"There may be another way," the spinner suggested. "On the mountain to the east, the one the locals call Razor, there is said to be a flower that burns eternally. Perhaps that will set the wheel ablaze."

"Very well," Tonsta agreed, replacing his tinder box. "How will I find it?"

"I've never seen it for myself, but I've been told it sits at the center of a lake, filled with gems. You must not take any of the gems, for if you do you shall turn to one yourself and sink to the bottom."

Tonsta thought that sounded outlandishly ridiculous, however, he had also thought the same of golden nuggets falling from the sky, so he said nothing of that. He was halfway out the window when the spinner called to him.

"You *will* come back, won't you?" There was a note of plea in his strange voice.

"I swore to lift the curse affecting the village. I don't intend to be made a liar." He didn't wait for the spinner to say more but lowered himself down the tower.

The trek to the mountain was arduous, and the path up it even more so. More than once Tonsta had to chuck his grappling hook in the air and use that to climb higher. This was quite clearly not a mountain that wanted visitors traipsing all over it.

It was quite dark by the time Tonsta reached the lake, but fortunately, it was just as the spinner had said, and he could see a single bright light flickering at the center of the lake.

He walked around the edge cautiously, marveling at the countless sparkling gems at the bottom. He thought briefly of reaching in to retrieve one, and how lovely it would look about Mother's neck, but he remembered the spinner's warning and resisted. On the far edge of the lake, he spotted a little boat bouncing along on its own, unmoored.

Since the spinner had said nothing of the safety of touching the water itself, Tonsta found a long stick on the bank and used it to catch the boat. It had an oar, and Tonsta pushed off the shore, shooting across the still water.

There was no ground beneath the fire-flower; instead it seemed to be growing from a skinny finger of crystal, poking up from the lake. Just as Tonsta was reaching out to grab it, sharp talons swooped down and snatched the flower from his grasp.

"Oh no!" Tonsta exclaimed, watching the burning flower vanish into the distance.

He rowed back to shore, his expression very sour indeed, wondering how he could possibly track the flower down.

"Why so glum, friend?" A squeaky voice spoke up at Tonsta's sleeve, and he leaped into the air.

A mouse sat beside him, nibbling on a piece of cheese it had presumably just stolen from Tonsta.

"That flower was my only chance to free someone and lift a curse from an entire town. Now I don't know what I shall do."

"Psh!" The mouse waved a paw. "I can get that flower back for you, easily! I know who took it."

Tonsta looked at the mouse doubtfully. It wasn't that he doubted the mouse's prowess as a thief, it was just that it seemed unlikely a mouse would voluntarily enter a bird's nest.

"Why would you help me?" he asked.

The mouse gobbled down the last of the stolen cheese and dusted off its paws.

"Why, out of the goodness of my heart of course!" it squeaked, then burst into chuckles. "No, no…I couldn't help but notice the size of your food stores, and I understand what an enormous weight that must be. I'll help you recover your bauble, and in exchange I'd be more than happy to relieve you of some of your burden."

Tonsta found it amusing that the mouse managed to structure the exchange in such a way that it sounded as though the mouse were doing him all the favors. But as he had little choice he agreed and the mouse scurried up onto his shoulder.

"Who took the fire?" he asked.

The mouse pointed across the lake at a distant peak sticking out of the clouds.

"That is where Aki, the raven who stole the fire, makes his nest. Doubtless the climb will be difficult, but you seem capable for a human."

Uncertain whether this was a compliment or not, Tonsta sighed and set off once more.

It took hours to reach the foot of the cliff, and Tonsta swapped tales with the mouse to pass the time. The mouse's tales were each more fantastical than the last. He fancied himself quite the adventurer and nodded condescendingly as Tonsta relayed the tale of the troll hag kidnapping Mother.

"Yes, yes…everyone knows troll hags routinely kidnap lovely maidens for their sons."

When they were finally staring up at the cliff, at the top of which the mouse assured Tonsta they would find the fire, Tonsta was exhausted and longing for a nap. However, the mouse was quite impatient and kept glancing pointedly at Tonsta's pack and rubbing his belly.

"How on earth will we get up that?" Tonsta sighed, studying the dense cloud above them.

"I saw a climbing hook and rope in your pack. Surely you know how to use it?" the mouse snapped.

Frowning, Tonsta set the pack on the ground to dig around in it. He did indeed have his climbing tackle, but he wasn't confident that the rock was safe enough to climb. He whipped the grappling hook up into the air and waited for it to fall back to earth. It found purchase and stuck fast, even as Tonsta yanked on it firmly and they began the ascent. They hit the clouds before they reached the hook, and when they emerged on the other side, they were chilled and damp.

The cliff wasn't nearly as tall as Tonsta had believed from below and when he reached the place where the hook was lodged, he only had to climb a few more yards to reach the top. There they found a cave just large enough for someone of Tonsta's height to enter. It was so dark that it was impossible to see beyond a few feet.

"This is it!" the mouse whispered. "If we're quiet about it, we might just catch him sleeping."

Wishing he could bring a light, Tonsta plunged into the darkness, feeling his way along the wall. Thankfully, the cave was not as deep as it seemed, and after turning a corner Tonsta saw a flickering light growing in the foreground. Around another corner they came upon the raven and Tonsta let out a small gasp. The bird which had stolen the fire was much larger than Tonsta had realized and he had no doubt that its wingspan was greater than the length of his entire body.

It was sat on a raised dais, almost as though it was holding court. Its eyes were tightly shut and a soft humming emanated from its beak. On a ribbon around its neck was the fire flower. It was flickering softly but clearly not bothering the bird. In the corner was a pile of alarmingly large bones. Clearly, rodents were not its only meat source.

"Now what?" Tonsta whispered to the mouse. When there was no answer, he glanced down at his shoulder. His heart sank; the mouse was not there. No doubt it had just used Tonsta to make the climb and it had its own plan.

He stepped cautiously towards the giant raven and his foot came crunching down on a bone. The bird's eyes snapped open, revealing one of them to be blood red.

"Who's there?" it croaked in a voice as evil as it looked.

Tonsta remained rooted to the spot and the bird rose from its perch, casting a monstrous shadow behind it.

"Come out!" the raven demanded. "Or are you too cowardly to face an old bird?"

Tonsta cleared his throat and stepped out of the tunnel into the flickering light cast by the fire flower.

"Good day!" he began brightly, bowing a little. His mouth felt very dry and his words came out somewhat raspy.

The bird tilted its head at him, evil red eye narrowed, waiting for him to continue. Tonsta had no idea how to go on. The entire plan had centered on stealing the fire flower, but he had not counted on it being around the bird's neck.

"Well, don't sniff the dust," the raven snapped. "You didn't climb up here for nothing. Did you come to steal my feathers? Or perhaps to kill me?"

"Oh no!" Tonsta exclaimed, shocked out of his silence. "My good sir, I was sent to retrieve the fire you now wear about your neck. If you wouldn't mind selling it, or perhaps trading it…." Tonsta let his voice trail off as the raven scrutinized him.

"Good sir?" the bird repeated, incensed. "My lad, I'll have you know that I am the emperor of all ravens. Aki the Ancient is my name and you would do well to remember it."

Tonsta bowed again, even lower, but the bird wasn't finished. It seemed to have forgotten it was old and frail.

"As for the fire, what do I need of gold? And what could you trade me of equal worth?"

Tonsta thought about everything he had in his pack, and his mind settled on the one item he had that might be worthy of trade. He reached into his tool satchel and drew out the Odin's Eye. The raven shrieked when it caught sight of the orb, flapping its wings and filling the chamber with a strong gust.

"That was stolen from me many years ago!" the raven insisted, its voice filled with rage.

Tonsta gulped, he didn't like the way the bird's red eye was studying him.

"I'm afraid I can't trade this, it was a gift."

"Ha!" The raven snorted.

Tonsta noticed a small movement on the bird's right side, and a moment later he saw the mouse sitting on the raven's back. It was gnawing on the ribbon.

"Return the Odin's Eye, and I *may* consider giving you the fire," the raven told him, eyes flashing dangerously.

The mouse held the fire in its front paws as it made a mad leap from the top of the raven's head, flying through the air towards Tonsta. The raven glanced up and snapped its beak at the mouse's tail, just barely missing it, and the mouse landed safely in Tonsta's outstretched hands.

"Run!" the mouse squeaked.

Tonsta didn't need to be told twice, and stuffing both the mouse and the fire in his tool satchel, he dashed into the dark tunnel. He could hear the giant bird fumbling around in the dark, and he felt tiny claws scratching up his tunic.

"Find somewhere to hide," the mouse told him. "I used some cord I found in your pack to tangle his feet, but it won't be long before he's freed himself."

Tonsta saw nowhere to hide on top of the cliff, so he lowered himself down the rope into the cloud and hugged the rock. Black wings swooped by, but the bird didn't seem to notice Tonsta huddled in the cloud. He waited a few more minutes, then descended to the bottom. The giant raven was nowhere to be seen.

"I thought you had abandoned me," Tonsta told the mouse.

"We made a deal!" The mouse looked quite affronted.

"Indeed we did," Tonsta replied, removing his pack and withdrawing his food parcel. He laid it open for the mouse. "Thank you for the help, my friend. Please, take whatever you wish."

The mouse sniffed around the food for a few moments, before taking hold of a large hunk of bread and an equally large piece of cheese. Tonsta marveled to see the small creature drag them off.

"Goodbye, and good luck in your endeavors!" the mouse called through a mouth stuffed with bread.

Tonsta watched his companion scamper off for a moment before he remembered that surely the raven would be returning at any moment.

When Tonsta reached the tower, it was near dawn and it was no longer raining gold. He wondered how long it had taken the frightened villagers to come out and collect it all. The spinner was dozing away even as the spinning wheel continued to churn out gold.

"Poor fellow," Tonsta thought sympathetically as he yawned.

He knelt beside the spinning wheel and drew the fire flower from his pocket. Since it wasn't burning in his pocket or his hand, Tonsta wasn't quite sure how to get it to work. Without really thinking about it, he blew on it as if it were an ember. Instantly, it brightened and shot out flaming little tendrils which wound their way up the spinning wheel until they had enveloped the thing.

The spinner awoke with a yelp as the spinning wheel released him, and his cloak caught fire, and Tonsta got his first look at the fellow he had risked so much to help. He was undoubtedly a troll, and an especially ugly one at that. A very short fellow, he was shaped rather like a knobbly potato and his mossy hair stood straight up from his head like a flame on a candle.

He danced on the spot, whacking at his smoldering cloak and shouting. He was so irate about it that he seemed to have missed the fact he was no longer a prisoner of the spinning wheel. When he finally stopped bouncing about, he looked at Tonsta and let out a shout of joy.

"Thank you! Friend, you have freed me!" He bowed very low so that his spud-like nose scraped the floor. "Take as much gold as you can carry."

With that, he turned his back on Tonsta and began to stuff his pockets full of gold coins and to wind up the thread which had fallen from him when the spinning wheel burnt up. Tonsta supposed he shouldn't have expected much more from a troll.

"Ahem!" He coughed, and the troll glanced up at him, a scowl clouding his eyes.

"Oh, you're still here," he said. "What else do you want? I've already offered you my gold."

Tonsta didn't like the troll's new tone, but he couldn't very well just let the fellow get trapped again.

"The sun will be up soon, and your cloak is burnt," Tonsta reminded him.

"Yes, yes," the troll replied absently, as he scurried around, coins spilling from between his fingers.

By the time the troll could carry no more, the sun was almost bursting through the trees. The troll was already prancing off through the thicket as Tonsta lowered himself out of the tower window for the last time. He heard the troll cackling gleefully as he trotted off, but a moment later he heard the sound of coins spilling. He turned just in time to see the troll jumping around trying to pick up his loot, before a ray of sun burst through the trees and froze the little fellow to the spot.

Tonsta sighed a little sadly as he walked up to the stone statue. The troll's face was frozen in delight and he was half bent towards the ground, one gold coin still in his hand. Tonsta gathered all the fallen coins into a bag and buried it under a nearby tree.

"Perhaps on my way home, I shall dig it up and bring it with me," he thought.

Back in the village, he was greeted with surprise and more than a few grumpy looks. He went straight up to the innkeeper and held out his hand.

"I'll take that payment now!" he declared.

"Pah! You must be joking," the innkeeper replied.

"Not at all," Tonsta said, lowering his hand. "If you go to the ruins, you will find the troll who brought the curse."

There was a great deal of murmuring around the room, not all of it pleased. It seemed as though some of the townspeople had become accustomed to the influx of gold and weren't entirely happy to see it go.

"I don't need my payment now," Tonsta said, seeing the grumpy faces, and thinking of the little sack of coins he had saved when burying the rest. "But when I return this way, I shall expect it." With that, he turned on his heel and marched out.

He had a long road ahead of him and many more adventures to find. He had already made one enemy, but he hoped to make new friends along the way.

Late in the fall Tonsta found himself on a little farm. The night was cold and biting, so he went to ask the farmer if he might sleep by his hearth. There was smoke piping out of the chimney and a delicious smell in the air. Tonsta's stomach rumbled as he knocked on the shiny painted door.

It was opened by a portly gentleman in red stockings, smoking a long pipe. He looked down at Tonsta in surprise as though expecting someone taller.

"Good evening friend!" Tonsta greeted him. "It's a cold night. I wonder if perhaps I might sleep in front of your fire tonight?"

The man's brow furrowed, and as he opened his mouth to reply, a plump woman appeared at his shoulder. She was well dressed and her shiny braids were wound around her head like a crown.

Clearly these farmers were very comfortable people.

"This lad is asking to sleep on the hearth tonight, my dear," the man told his wife, stepping aside so that she might take up the bulk of the door.

The woman looked Tonsta up and down, taking in his patched little boots and his weather-stained jacket. His red cap alone was the only item of clothing which still retained its original color. The expression on her face stated only too clearly that she didn't like the look of him, and her mouth curved a little in distaste.

"We have no room," she told Tonsta, her tone no warmer than the air outside. "If you wish, you can sleep in the barn but mind you don't upset the animals." She turned to close the door.

Tonsta stuck his lip out and turned his gaze to the farmer. The man looked sympathetic, but not enough to overrule his wife. He held up a finger, indicating that Tonsta should wait a moment, then disappeared behind the door. A moment later he returned and handed Tonsta a worn old blanket. Heavy flakes began to fall as Tonsta trudged towards the barn.

The cow looked up as Tonsta entered but said nothing and shut her eyes once more. Tonsta sighed heavily as he unwrapped his light food parcel and took stock of its contents. All that remained was a hunk of stale bread, a few nibbles of cheese, and a few sips of milk.

"That is sad fare, friend. It is sadder still to find oneself lacking any food."

Tonsta sat bolt upright and peered around the barn for the speaker. He found him sitting on the opposite side of the cow, half hidden in the shadows. He looked like a very small person, perhaps the size of a child, but Tonsta was certain he could see a long, pointed beard reaching to the fellow's belt.

"So it is," Tonsta replied cautiously. "Would you like to share my meal?"

The little man hopped off the overturned bucket he'd been sitting on and ducked underneath the cow to reach Tonsta. In the dim light, Tonsta could just make out a red cap on the stranger's head.

"What a fine lad you are to offer!" the little man said, accepting the bread Tonsta was holding out. He gobbled it down quickly while Tonsta was still savoring his half. "Perhaps a sip or two of milk to wash it down?" he asked.

A tad miffed, but not unkind, Tonsta handed the little man the bottle which he drained almost instantly.

Tonsta swallowed the last of the bread and began to stow the food parcel away.

"This isn't enough! Not nearly enough for the two of us," the little man said. "Be a good lad and fetch more food from the sack."

"There is no more," Tonsta said, opening the bag to show the man.

But the little fellow merely smiled a bit impishly and cocked his head at Tonsta.

"Are you sure of that? Perhaps you should have another look."

Annoyed, and wondering what on earth this little man was playing at, Tonsta plunged his arm into the sack, expecting to disappear up to the elbow as he reached for the bottom. Instead his hand met something solid. He emptied the sack out in front of the stranger, setting out a roast bird, a loaf of much fresher bread, a cake of cheese, and a full bottle of milk. The little man had no reaction to the look of astonishment on Tonsta's face, but cracked his knuckles and said, "Well now, let's eat."

Tonsta narrowed his eyes at the stranger and didn't touch the food, despite the growling of his stomach. The cow had opened her eyes up once more and seemed to be watching the exchange with mild interest.

"What manner of person are you?" Tonsta asked the little man.

"What a rude question!" the fellow exclaimed. "You don't hear me asking you that despite how ridiculous you look." He didn't seem truly offended however, and Tonsta could almost see his eyes twinkling mischievously.

Tonsta cautiously took a bite of the chicken. It tasted wonderful! And quite real. He dug in enthusiastically, and the little man sat back with an impish grin. When Tonsta was quite full, he began gathering up the leftovers to put back into the sack, and to his surprise he found that it was already full. He shot a glance at the little man who was sitting cross-legged, patting the cow affectionately and whispering to it.

"I expected I would be sleeping in a cold barn on an empty stomach tonight," he told the man. "Please, friend, tell me to whom do I owe my full belly?"

The little man straightened his red cap and stroked his beard. He shrugged.

"I've gone by many names. Tonight 'friend' suits me well enough." He patted the cow, who turned her head and gave Tonsta a long look.

"Quite a warm reception the farmer's wife gave you, eh? Better than I'd have given you if you'd been a selfish, ungrateful lad."

There was a soft rumbling sound from somewhere near Tonsta's feet, and something warm and fuzzy rubbed against his ankles. He jumped and looked down at the sleek grey cat. It blinked slowly at him and leapt into the little man's lap, where it lapped at a bowl of milk that had certainly not been there a moment before. The pieces were beginning to click in Tonsta's mind and suddenly the answer struck him.

"You're the Tomten!" he exclaimed, more than a little frightened, for although he had faced trolls, and giant ravens, the tale of the Tomten had been drummed into him at an early age, and he knew the Tomten was not one to take rudeness lightly.

"Indeed!" The Tomten puffed his chest out proudly. "Or rather *a* Tomten. There are a number of us."

Tonsta tried to reconcile what he remembered of the stories with the events of that evening and hit a snag.

"Are you the patron of this farm then?" The farmers had not seemed the sort of people who would respect the Tomten.

"They are a prickly sort for sure," the Tomten replied, as if he read Tonsta's thoughts, his eyes glinting dangerously. "But they wouldn't dare offend *me*." His tone spoke volumes and Tonsta shivered thinking of what tales were told of the Tomten's anger. "They've never forgotten the pat of butter since, I can assure you of that."

Tonsta knew he was referring to the butter which tomtens preferred on their Christmas porridge. The Tomten continued to stroke the sleek little cat, who purred loudly and nestled against him. The cow was gazing fondly at the group, blinking sleepily.

"So, you care for the animals, just like the stories say?" Tonsta asked.

"More or less," the Tomten replied. "Sometimes when I'm feeling especially benevolent, I'll help out with the farm work after everyone has gone to bed. Sometimes, when the farmer's wife has been particularly unpleasant, I'll put sawdust in her stockings, or pinch her nose till it turns blue!" The Tomten cackled, and Tonsta was again glad that the little fellow had taken a liking to him.

"But you're a good lad," the Tomten continued. "Your parents raised you to have proper manners, so I promise I won't pinch your nose in the night, nor will I steal your shoes."

Tonsta thanked him profusely and the Tomten waved it off as though it were nothing, which of course it wasn't.

"If you return this way come Christmas time, I may even share my porridge with you." And with that the Tomten scooped up the cat and trudged out into the night.

The next morning Tonsta awoke to find himself sleeping against the cow, with the cat curled up against his chest. There was fresh powder on the ground, completely unmarred, save for the prints of the cat and those of a very small person.

Tonsta and the Bridegroom

A few days into winter, Tonsta found himself in a merry little town all abuzz with the impending arrival of a prince, who was betrothed to the local earl's daughter. Even Tonsta got caught up in the excitement. He had been wearing the same little boots and worn jacket since he began his travels, and so he decided to stay awhile and have a new set of clothes made. He wouldn't be too disappointed if he got to see the wedding as well.

So, on the day that the prince was to arrive, Tonsta was gathered in the street with everyone else, wearing his new red stockings and shiny new shoes. He also had new blue britches and a matching jacket, and of course his little red hat.

Little children pushed each other aside to get a good look at the procession and girls swooned at the sight of the prince. Tonsta stood on tiptoe trying to get a look, but people kept pushing into him. Just as the group was almost out of sight, Tonsta found himself shoved to the front of the bystanders with an uninhibited view of the prince.

Tonsta gasped as he saw the great beast sitting on his miserable looking horse, grinning like a mouse with cheese and waving his shovel sized hand at the onlookers.

The troll had clearly tried sprucing himself up for the occasion, for his mossy hair was flattened in a fashion which suggested it had met a comb. He was also dressed a little nicer than most trolls, wearing a scarlet cloak and a gaudy ruby on a gold chain.

The procession went around the corner out of sight, leaving Tonsta feeling a little sick thinking of the earl's poor daughter.

"I must find a way to stop this," he thought to himself, glancing at the overcast sky, which must be protecting the hideous creature from the sun's rays. He glanced up and down the street, looking for anyone who might be having a similar reaction, but all he saw were dazed faces and glassy eyes. "This whole town is in a stupor!" he exclaimed.

He had heard the wedding was to take place the following day, and so he determined to put a stop to it before the night was out. In his new clothes, all clean and shiny, Tonsta could very easily pass for a servant in the earl's house, and he managed to sneak in through the kitchens without drawing much attention. He *did* get noticed by the blustering red-faced cook as he was going by, and a pitcher of mead and a tray of sweets were shoved into his arms.

Holding his tray, Tonsta navigated the dining hall, invisible as a ghost. He kept one eye trained on the head table the entire time, taking note of the glum face on the earl's daughter. She didn't seem petrified by her betrothed, so Tonsta assumed that she, like everyone else, was under some sort of spell.

For his part, the troll stuffed himself, drank and laughed, clearly enjoying himself thoroughly.

"What a distasteful sight," Tonsta muttered as he set his empty tray down in the corner.

"Isn't it though? Such a frightful creature, and it's making quite a stench in the hall."

Tonsta looked around for the speaker and his eyes rested on a large fluffy cat. She blinked slowly at him, as though judging whether he was intelligent enough to understand her.

"Are we the only ones who see him for what he is?" Tonsta asked her.

The cat stretched, stalking up to Tonsta's ankles and rubbing against them.

"As far as I've seen," she replied. "The milkmaids were all gaga over it, they actually thought it was *handsome*. Pah! As if something that so closely resembles a potato could be handsome." She glanced up at Tonsta. "No offense dear."

Tonsta hadn't been offended until she added that last part but was too preoccupied to dwell on it.

"Hang on…What makes us special?"

The cat gazed at Tonsta stoically and sniffed him for a moment. She sneezed.

"*I* can see it because I'm not as easily fooled as you humans! As for you, there's some sort of magic aura hanging about your person; it has an almost *ancient* smell to it." She narrowed her eyes.

"Of course!" Tonsta thought, almost smacking himself in the head. The Odin's Eye must give some sort of clear-sightedness to the possessor.

"How can we put a stop to this?" he asked her, changing the subject.

"Why must you?" The cat asked. "It's terribly amusing."

"My mother raised me to be a good Christian lad who helps those in need," Tonsta replied huffily.

The cat watched the scene at the head table for a moment before replying. It seemed to Tonsta she wasn't truly interested in remedying the situation so much as reveling in the unpleasantness of it.

"The way I see it, the spell must be on its person, not the town itself," the cat said finally.

"Why?" Tonsta asked, uncertain if that was a good thing or not.

"I don't know! It seems easier," the cat replied huffily. "If you're going to question me then you can just take care of this mess by yourself."

Tonsta apologized profusely which seemed to soothe the cat's ruffled feelings. Her plan was to sneak into the troll's room after everyone had gone to sleep and search his belongings for the enchanted object. It seemed a simple enough plan, although Tonsta wasn't thrilled with the idea of searching a sleeping troll.

"I'll be the lookout," the cat offered when Tonsta voiced his concerns.

That night, after the last of the revelers was slumbering in his bed, Tonsta and the cat crept into the troll's room. The troll was snoring fit to fell a forest, and his malodorous breath filled the room. The cat leapt to the foot of the bed and fixed the sleeping troll with her yellow eyes while Tonsta searched the room.

The troll had brought very little of his own belongings and it took Tonsta mere minutes to search every nook and cranny of the room.

"There's nothing here," Tonsta whispered to the cat. He was beginning to fear the cat's assumption was wrong.

The cat merely blinked slowly and flicked her gaze between the troll and Tonsta. Heart sinking, Tonsta understood the cat's meaning perfectly. The troll still wore the giant ruby around his neck.

"Of course," Tonsta sighed gloomily.

Unfortunately, it wasn't just a simple matter of slipping the chain over the troll's head. The creature had sunk so heavily into the bed that the frame was bowing almost to the floor. Tonsta stood on tiptoes and stretched but the ruby was just out of reach. He spotted a piece of kindling on the hearth and for several fruitless minutes he tried to hook the gem. Finally, he resigned himself to clambering up on the bed.

The troll snorted as Tonsta stepped over his arm but didn't move. Tonsta pulled one of his special tools out of his tool satchel, and carefully lifted the ruby off of the troll, never taking his eyes off the creature's face. As quietly as he could he snipped the links of the gold chain, freeing the ruby. With a silent dance of celebration Tonsta and the cat fled the room, in possession of what they hoped was disguising the troll.

The next morning Tonsta helped in the kitchens once more, watching the doors to the great hall carefully and listening for the sounds of panic he expected. To Tonsta's dismay the troll strutted into the great hall as bold as brass, wrapped in his scarlet cloak and grinning from ear to ear.

"You've noticed that our nighttime jaunt seems to have been for nothing, I see."

Tonsta looked around and spotted the cat cleaning herself in a patch of sunlight streaming through an open door.

The ceremony began shortly after noon. The only person who looked more miserable than the bride was Tonsta. He felt as though he had let everyone down.

The troll had insisted the wedding be held in the great hall rather than in a Christian church as was proper, so many people had crowded in to watch the spectacle, Tonsta amongst them. He found himself squished at the back watching the proceedings glumly beside two kitchen maids.

As the ceremony commenced and it was nearly time for the vows, a thought struck him. The troll was wearing the same scarlet cloak he had worn the day before! He knew what he must do now, but how could he possibly get close enough to enact his plan?

"Friend!" he whispered to the cat, who looked up from her washing near the door. "I have an idea, but you must trust me.…"

As the speaker drew to a close and the bride began to recite her vows, Tonsta tucked his little tinder box back into his tool satchel and watched anxiously for any sign that his plan had worked. Soon enough he saw a wisp of smoke rising from the floor at the head of the great hall and a fluffy tail whisking out of sight. A moment later the red cloak was enveloped in flames and with a yelp the troll tore it off dancing around and smacking himself as he attempted to extinguish the flames.

Cries of horror rose throughout the hall as everyone saw the "prince" for what he truly was.

The earl's daughter shrieked and dove behind her father. With a howl of rage the troll ran from the hall. People scattered out of his way and let him flee without contest.

Tonsta felt a swish at his feet and reached down to pet the cat.

"Nicely done," he told her. The cat purred affectionately.

"Poor thing," she commented. "I suppose at best it just wanted to be loved, and at worst it wanted power over all these deceived humans."

Tonsta considered these words in silence. Whatever the troll's intentions were, they would never know.

Tonsta and the Christmas Spruce

The day before Christmas Tonsta found himself trudging through knee deep snow in the mountains. He had no idea which mountains, for all the locals he had spoken to seemed to have different names for them. They ranged from; "Harsh Queen", to "Hag's Demise", to "Dragon's Jaws". None of these names inspired a feeling of safety or of comfort but Tonsta couldn't pass up the challenge. So here he was, the day before Christmas, cold, hungry and tired.

He paused on a ledge, huffing and puffing, to enjoy the view. The sun was getting low on the horizon and breaking through the clouds in radiant beams. From his perch he could see the last town he had been in and ahead a new town, nestled in a valley many miles below. Smoke puffed from the tiny chimneys and the light from hundreds of candles glowed faintly. It looked warm and inviting.

"What luck!" he said to himself rubbing his mittens together. "If I make good time, perhaps I shall reach it before supper."

He set off with renewed energy but all too soon a snow storm descended, blinding him and hiding the path. Giant flakes beat against his face, diving down his throat with each breath and stealing the air from his lungs.

Frightened of losing the path, or worse, falling off of it, Tonsta eagerly dove into the first alcove he found. It wasn't a deep cave, or even completely sheltered from the elements. Snow lay a foot deep almost to the back of it. Several little trees were clustered by the entrance and Tonsta thought perhaps he would break some branches off for a fire.

Just as he was getting his little hatchet out, the branches began to quiver.

"Oi! That's unnecessary, I'll come out peacefully!"

The branches continued to shake violently, as though whoever was in there was stuck, and Tonsta scooted as far back as he could in the tight space. A moment later a medium sized troll dressed in patched multicolored furs tumbled out of the branches. He glowered at Tonsta, as though he were at fault for his being stuck in the tree and plopped down as far from the boy as he could.

"What do you think you're doing, sneaking up on a fellow with a hatchet?" the troll asked. "At least have the decency to get a fellow when he's awake."

A little offended at the insinuation of bad sportsmanship, Tonsta replied in an equally huffy tone.

"My good—troll, I had no idea you were in there. I was merely planning on starting a fire."

The troll eyed him suspiciously, eyes darting between Tonsta's face and the hatchet. He wiped his bulbous nose and crossed his arms.

"Suppose I believe that's true for a moment," the troll said. "This is *my* cave. I found it first. If anyone is going to be building a fire it will be me! You can just scurry along before I decide to eat you."

Tonsta glanced at the dim sky outside, wondering if there was enough remaining light to catch in the Odin's eye. It seemed a bit uncharitable to use considering the troll was offering *not* to eat him.

"If you had the tools to start a fire you would have done so already, instead of curling up in a tree against the elements," Tonsta decided, planting himself cross-legged on the cave floor.

The troll scowled but sat and watched Tonsta suspiciously as he trimmed some branches from the trees and got a fire going.

Once the fire was blazing away and both occupants of the cave were a little warmer, Tonsta felt comfortable striking up a conversation.

"Now look here," he began. "I know you and I got off to a bad start, and you'd probably like to eat me once I fall asleep, but there's no need. I'm more than willing to share my dinner with you, provided you promise not to try and trick me, harm me, or do anything that will end with me on a spit over the fire." He held out his hand.

Reluctantly, the troll gave Tonsta one of his fingers and they shook. A boy of his word, Tonsta dug out his food parcel and gave the troll a leg of mutton. After that the troll was a good deal less sulky and said no more of eating Tonsta. Instead, he told Tonsta how he had wound up in that cave.

The troll, who called himself Dunkan, lived high up in the mountains and had been down in the forest making black market deals.

This piqued Tonsta's curiosity, for he had always known certain trolls preferred different regions, but the existence of an underground market was news to him. What sort of contraband could they be dealing with?

On the way back up the mountain Dunkan had lost his footing and his bag containing that week's food for him and his family. It had fallen into a crevice a few feet from the cave. While Dunkan was bemoaning its loss, and trying to decide what to do, the storm had descended and shortly after that Tonsta had appeared.

"What unfortunate luck!" Tonsta exclaimed sympathetically. The idea that Dunkan, this large stump-like creature, had a family at home waiting for him, struck a bit of a cord. Never before had it occurred to Tonsta that trolls had families, although he felt foolish now admitting it to himself. To comfort himself, he remembered that the trolls he had dealt with in the past were quite clearly malevolent creatures. It also occurred to him that Dunkan might be fabricating the entire thing to obtain sympathy. He told Dunkan of his travels but left out the stories pertaining to trolls and their demise at his hands.

"What a fitting night for a truce between our kinds, eh?" Tonsta commented lightly.

"Is it an important night?" Dunkan asked, for trolls of course do not celebrate the birth of our Lord.

So Tonsta told Dunkan the Christmas story and by the end the troll's eyes had gone a bit misty. He also told Dunkan what he was missing at home on this night.

"I suppose my brothers felled a big spruce, and mother baked her Christmas bread. The house looks very fine decked with cedar boughs."

Dunkan must have heard the note of sadness in Tonsta's voice for he replied, "That sounds very fine and comfortable, but see here we have a spruce of our own." He waved his large hand at the tree they had all but stripped bare for their fire.

"Indeed," Tonsta laughed. "Why it's even decorated!" The tree was lightly dusted in snow.

Dunkan curled up next the fire, commenting that he had to be up early to get home, and thanked Tonsta not to push him off the cliff in the night. There was a twinkle in his eyes as he said it.

Tonsta lay awake, not only because he didn't completely trust Dunkan, but also because something was nagging at him. Finally, after tossing another branch on the fire Tonsta grabbed his rope and headed out of the cave. The storm had died down and revealed a clear crisp night with all the stars out.

It took only a few minutes to discover the crevice which Dunkan's sack had fallen into and Tonsta set to work securing his climbing ax in the snow. He lowered himself down carefully, feeling slightly claustrophobic as the hole began to swallow him. The sack was almost invisible buried in the fresh snow brought by the storm. Tonsta dug it out and was surprised by the size of it. It was almost as big as he was and a lot heavier than he'd anticipated. It presented a slight problem in ascending the rope once more. Finally, he decided to tie it to the end of the rope and climb back up. As he neared the top however, he felt the anchor giving way and he began to fall. Panicking, he yelled desperately, "Oi friend!"

Faster than Tonsta would have thought possible, the troll's face appeared at the top of the hole. The surprised troll grabbed the anchor before it slipped over the edge and effortlessly hauled the little boy out of the hole, bringing the sack up last of all.

"Merry Christmas!" Tonsta gasped, shoving the heavy bag towards the troll.

Mixed emotions crossed Dunkan's hideous face and great big tears welled in his eyes.

"Thank you!" he exclaimed taking the sack and holding it as though it were his child. "You know, for a human you aren't a bad lad…." He seemed as though he might like to add more but instead, he set the sack down and rummaged around in it for a moment or two. When he emerged, he was holding a tiny silver bell. He gazed at it for a moment and then handed it to Tonsta.

"Hold this bell to your ear, and you will be able to hear the voices of whoever it is you wish to hear, be it nearby or faraway."

With that, the troll heaved his bag back over his shoulder and took off down the trail, quite clearly eager to get home now that he had his sack.

"Thank you!" Tonsta shouted at his retreating back.

Grinning to himself, Tonsta went back into the cave and settled down next to the fire. Holding the bell up to his ear he thought of his family and of how much he missed them. He let out a shout of joy as, just as the troll had said, the voices of his mother and brothers sounded in his ear as clear as a bell.

Feeling warm and comforted on the inside for the first time in a long time, Tonsta curled up beside the fire and closed his eyes.

www.ingramcontent.com/pod-product-compliance
Lightning Source LLC
Chambersburg PA
CBHW022108050726
47591CB00002B/720